DATE DUE

FOLLETT

Because Amelia Smiled

To you: Pass it on!

Library of Congress Cataloging-in-Publication Data is available. Library of Congress Catalog Card Number 2011046622. ISBN 978-0-7636-4169-6 Printed in Shenzhen, Guangdong, China. This book was typeset in Gararond. The illustrations were done in pencil, water soluble crayon, and watercolor. Candlewick Press, 99 Dover Street, Somerville, Massachusetts 02144. Visit us at www.candlewick.com 12 13 14 15 16 17 CCP 10 9 8 7 6 5 4 3 2 1

Because Amelia Smiled

DAVID EZRA STEIN

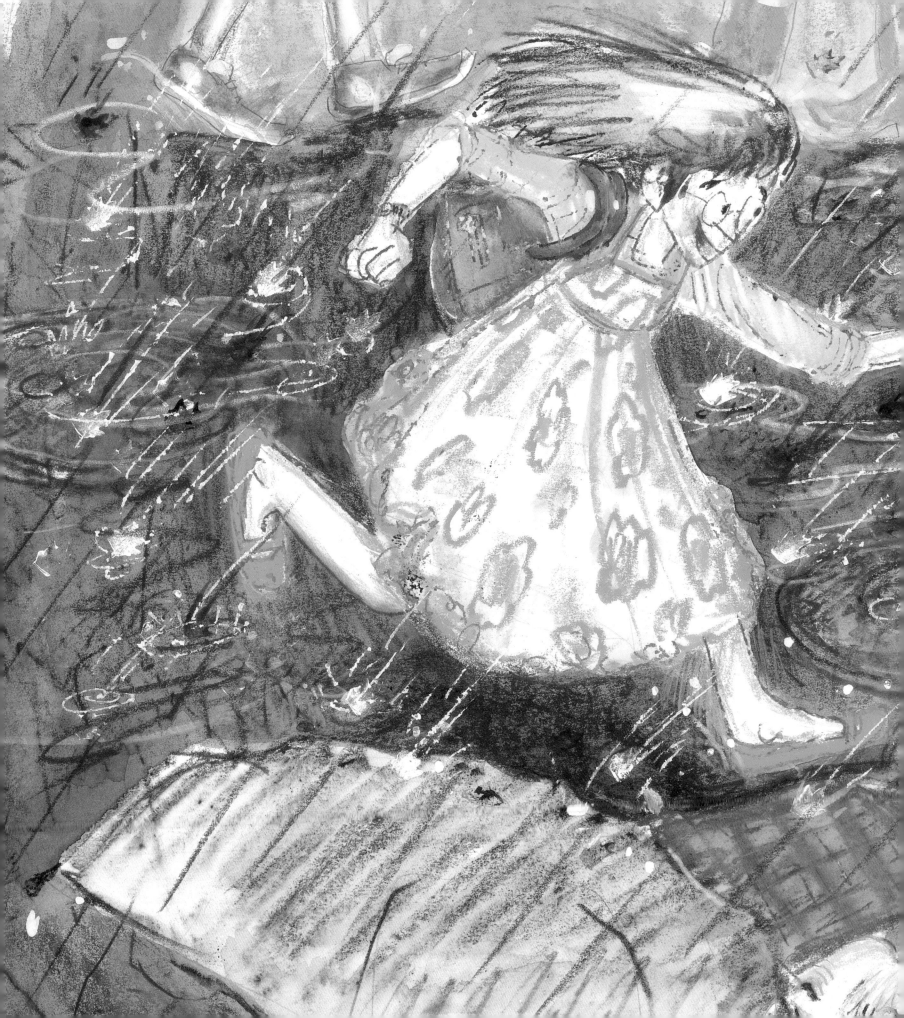

Because Amelia smiled, coming down the street . . .

Mrs. Higgins smiled, too.

She thought of her grandson, Lionel, in Mexico
and baked some cookies to send to him.

Because Mrs. Higgins baked cookies . . .

Lionel ate one of the cookies.

He decided to share the rest with his class . . .

and teach them an English song about cookies.

Because Lionel taught his class a song . . .

one of his students, kickboxer Sensacia Golpes,
decided to be a teacher, too.

She had her cousin record her in the plaza
and put the video online.

Zesta Crump and her ballet club in England saw the video and decided to add some new moves to their goodwill recital . . .

in Israel.

Kotz Gluberman, age four, who was in the audience, decided he liked dancing after all.

in Paris.

The band felt so fancy, they gave a free show on the Pont Neuf. On the barge below, Gregor the ex-clown listened and sighed. Their love song "Con Corazón Intacto" reminded him of his old flame, the Amazing Phyllis, who lived in Positano, Italy.

Phyllis was so happy, she threw roses from a high wire. She was caught on film by a TV crew that was doing a story on stray cats.

Back in New York, Lydia Frittata saw Phyllis on TV while making pizzas on Carmine Street.

On the subway home, she began a scarf of roses for her niece, Pia Maria. She sat across from Pigeon Man Jones.

He watched her and remembered his dear old grandma,
who loved to knit.

When he got back to his rooftop and let his pigeons out, he wondered if maybe somehow, wherever Grandma was, she could see them.

Because Pigeon Man Jones let his birds out,
Amelia saw them . . .

and she smiled.